The Nine Principles Of Power

The Secret Sauce to Ultimate Success

By

Gary E. Barthelmy

Dedication

I want to dedicate this book to my elementary school teacher, who first challenged me to read more, and to my high school English teacher, Miss Williams, who predicted that I would write a book one day. And to my sister Monette Theloma for all the work that she's done to never give up on me and my father Barthelmy Saint Thelmy for being a great man that he was despite however many children he had he still made time for me. To my mother Julienne ENNEUS for teaching how to lead at an easy age. May you rest in peace.

To the USF Sarasota-Manatee staff, Dr. James Unever, Dr. Gi, and Dr. Ngo, for taking their time to work with me during my struggle with statistics to obtain a master's degree in criminal justice administration, despite the challenges I was facing. Also, I want to thank Dr. Unever for selecting me for the outstanding undergraduate research award. I want to dedicate this book to the Sarasota Herald Tribune's Elizabeth Dijenis for putting me on the front page to showcase my challenges, and when I graduate with my master's degree, I want to say thank you to all of you for all the great work and for not giving up on me. Because they believed in me, I was able to believe in myself. I want to dedicate this book to the division of the blinds for accepting me into the business enterprise program to be able to run a business. Furthermore, I want to dedicate this book to the Lighthouse of Broward for giving me the chance to understand that being blind was not the end of the world.

Acknowledgment

I want to say thank you to all of you for all the adversities that I faced in drafting this book. I also want to say to all the adversities that I faced in this life, "Thank you for giving me the chance to write this book." Because without those adversities, I wouldn't be writing this book this way. Those adversities are what made me who I am today. Because of them, I was able to do the work and see that regardless of your adversities, you should never give up. I want to say thank you to my two sons, Murduq and Michael, for always being there for me, always believing in me, and always telling me that I'm a great father. Thank you, and thank you again tomorrow. Both of my ex-wives and I have learned something new from you guys every day.

Table Of Contents

Preface

How often have you asked yourself questions such as these:

Have I achieved so far what I have wanted to achieve?
If I had a disability, would it hinder my success?
Do I believe in good things?

If you have asked some of these questions to yourself, then this right here may be the best read for you. This book includes my personal experiences, detailing what I learned from a major event that turned my life upside-down. There was one particular moment of truth that made me decide my future.

I struggled through my childhood. I had a rare condition that made me speak backward. I was bullied at school by older kids who treated me badly, not only inside but also outside the school. Getting bullied, especially at school, is the first step toward breaking down the personality of a growing child, whose impact can either be positive or negative. The bullied child will either adopt all of those bad habits and become a menace, or he will hate them all and follow a decent path. I was fortunate enough to not assume bad habits from the bullying scenario at my school.

My years in high school were also not a walk in the park. From being a teenager until today, I was a corrections officer—the phase was filled with headaches and toughies. Through all of this, I never lost hope in life. However, something happened so instantly that it turned my life upside-down. There were times that I thought that life was over for me. I had lost everything, and there was no will to survive. Just when I had decided to finish myself off, a ray of hope came through that brought along a new outlook on life. I made use of my disabilities and continued living a normal life. I never gave up and expected good things from the future, which is why I was able to achieve my goals.

Through this book, I hope to motivate and encourage my readers to never give up. The book also brings forth an emotional rollercoaster ride, where I pen my personal experiences from real life and how I dealt with them. I hope that my encounters with life will help the readers rise again with an endeavor to achieve what they want, because it is never too late.

Chapter 1
How to Rise Above All Odds

"You learn to rise above a lot of bad things that happen in your life. And you have to keep going."
-Lauren Bacall

    Some incidents in your life leave a mark on you by breaking or deforming you in any way. But you never know that at the very moment these events tear you apart, they somehow bring forth the best version of you. The same happened to me. An incident changed my life and showed the world an entirely different version of Gary Ernneus. Today, I am content with myself, and there are no regrets left in life.

I was born into a somewhat corporate couple, where both my father and mother were business people. My parents were both entrepreneurs and also philanthropists. They liked to help people in need by feeding them and providing them with the things they needed. They were both happy people and made others laugh as well. My father was a spiritual man, except for the fact that he had many kids from multiple women. He had almost 15 children, of whom I was maybe the 10th. However, on my mother's side, I am the third out of five children. I had good relationships with my siblings from my mother's side. In fact, on my father's side, all of the siblings were scattered.

Despite having a trail of children behind, my father never forgot his responsibilities on me. He always came on time to pick me up from school. He never refused to take out time for other kids and for me. He taught me the fundamentals of business and several other things in life. The bond between us got stronger as we shared everything.

On the other hand, my mother was a bit different from me. She was in the trading business and met my father during a business deal. She was short heighted, probably 5 feet tall. People around her loved her presence simply because she made them happy. She also loved to help others and always tried to take care of the needy. She fed the strangers and helped poor people who needed support. Anyone who encountered my mom would say that she was a great person.

My mother went into a coma after giving birth to me for 27 days. I was a motherless child during this period. No one knew if she was going to survive or not. But she came back on the 28th day. I was then handed over to her to be fed and taken care of. As time passed and I grew older, I realized that my mother was not always there for her children. She loved us, but she cared more about her work. Her buying and selling business took her to places because of which she let her kids in the hands of nannies and babysitters. It felt horrible to be fed by other people, because sometimes some of them turned out to be inappropriate for the job. My mother was the kind of person who would not really talk to us much, but she made sure that we were getting everything we wanted. Nonetheless, she never knew that a mother's love surpasses all.

Staying unattended by the most desired people at home, my parents, let me go through a little bit of anxiety at a very young age, which is why I later on somehow developed a condition called dyslexia. Having to deal with dyslexia was frustrating, as it became my most significant problem as a kid. It is a condition in which people (mostly children) find difficulty in reading, writing, spelling, and speaking. I had a problem understanding the mathematical equations because when I looked at the numbers, I used to answer backward. This was because my brain used to process the information faster than I spoke.

Coping with dyslexia was one of the toughest phases of my life. I would get angry at myself for not being able to read or understand the given instructions. I had no idea what it meant to be able to do things this way. I used to curse myself for always being late compared to other kids. I was a left-handed kid, but at school, I was forced to write with my right hand. I was pressured the whole time by my family, school and society that it was something wrong to be a lefty. As a result, I learned how to write with both hands at the same time. It was really very frustrating dealing with dyslexia. It is something that, until now, I was ashamed of. I didn't want anyone to know about it, as it felt erroneous somewhere deep down inside me. The pressure from the outside world suppressed me to the extent that I became complex and didn't even trust myself for anything. I underestimated myself for not being able to do anything in the world. I felt like a loser. There were times that even if I knew that I was answering a math equation correctly, I would read it again and again to make sure that my answer was correct. None of this was easy to handle, and my struggle with dyslexia continued.

However, at last, my fight with dyslexia led me to develop the habit of reading. I started reading more and more when I was in the 3rd grade. I became so efficient at reading that I began reading two categories above my level in two years. My teachers noticed my ability to be a step ahead at reading than other students, and so they appreciated me. I discovered this habit of reading after I won a contest in school. It was a vocabulary word competition that none of the students was able to pronounce do well. And so I was the one who won the contest. It was the time when I realized the importance of reading—not specifically books but anything. My love for books and reading material grew more prominent as I wanted to live inside the library because, to me, it was the best place in the world that comforted me. I would also sometimes read outside the classroom and even before going to the class, which made me better prepared for the lectures than the other students. The one most important thing that I learned from developing my habit of reading was that it doesn't matter what adversities you are going through in your life; the more you practice, the more it will train you to get better at anything you want.

At the age of 10, I got bullied at school by older kids. Those children used to tease me because of the way I spoke, as I stuttered a little while reading. One day, I saw a few girls coming toward me after school. The next thing they did was, they pushed me against the wall and pulled my bag pack, dumped it on the ground and stomped on it. I was lying on the ground, crying, and I could see all of them laughing at me for the fact that I read backward. I was so embarrassed, I picked up my books, put them back in my bag, and went home crying.

Another time, an older boy in school named David teamed up with other boys to pick a fight with me after school. So, what they did was gather around me as I was coming out of the school's gate. I was shocked and afraid of what they were going to do to me in the next moment. Out of nowhere, one of the boys came forward and punched me hard in the face. I fell on the ground then and there, while everyone else around me started laughing at me. David and those other boys dropped me on the ground and punched me almost 50 times, but I didn't give up. I hit him harder to fight him back until they all went away themselves. I didn't know where that courage came from at that very moment, that let me raise my hand against him and stand for my defense. Maybe it was because I didn't want to be left with the same feeling I had that day when I got humiliated by those girls. It felt awful to be declared a loser.

I couldn't bear to feel the pain again. After a few days, I came across David again, but this time I confronted him fearlessly and stared him right in the eyes. I was confident and unafraid, and I didn't care about the consequences. All I was concerned about at that time was facing my distress. The next time I encountered David's bullying act, I defended myself by fighting him back, as I had been practicing fight moves by watching karate movies or anything that dealt with defensive fighting. I used to watch Bruce Lee's films, and it was from there. I learned how to defeat the bad guys. I learned that even if you are the underdog, all you need is the will to train yourself to overcome anything. So, yes, at this point, I would like to accept the fact that I was an underdog, and the fear of my inner limitations crowded me. However, when I taught myself how to face my fears, I was able to overcome the obstacles by never giving up. I trained myself physically and intellectually to never be afraid to challenge the bullies.

I learned to fight back when bullied. I learned that if you know how to stand up for your own rights, no one can let you down. This positive notion affected me both mentally and physically, turning me into a confident person and not a loser. The next time I went through the neighborhood or the hallway in school, the kids used to look up to me because I had been able to stand up for myself. They saw my struggle to fight the bullying and face my fears, and from that moment onward, I made it my mission to fight for those who were unable to fight for themselves.

I never told my parents about being bullied at school, as I felt ashamed of it. No one in my house, not even my siblings, knew what I was going through. I thought anyone who would hear about me being bullied would laugh at me for not being able to fight back for myself. The only thing I did as a reaction to that bullying was to go inside my shell, lock myself up in my room, and learn how to fight back.

I learned how to confront my fears and not run away from them. It didn't matter how old those kids were compared to me; I was later able to challenge them to the spelling contest. I even countered them by speaking better than them. The day I got the courage to fight for my rights, it never mattered to me how big the problem was; I dealt with it with nerve. It was the best feeling in the world.

The most important way I overcame all of the struggles in my primary school was that I never restricted myself to a specific thing. I spread my boundaries and explored every corner. I never depended on anyone and taught myself how to read, write, and speak despite fighting with dyslexia. I never limited my reading skills to a specific material or genre; in fact, I gave way to anything that was in hand. I read everything, from newspapers to school textbooks. I always kept a dictionary with me to look up the difficult words that I didn't understand. I was never hesitant to ask questions to anyone as I had this hunger for knowledge.

I never lost hope, as I found light even in the dark. It didn't matter how disabled I was to write, read or speak; I still struggled myself uphill to the right path. Never make your disabilities or your insecurities an obstacle to success, as in the words of Stephen Hawking. However, this was only the first phase of my battle toward achieving the best, no matter what state I was in. There is still a long way to go.

Chapter 2

The Power of Patience and

Grace

"We could never learn to be brave and patient, if there were only joy in the world."
-Helen Keller

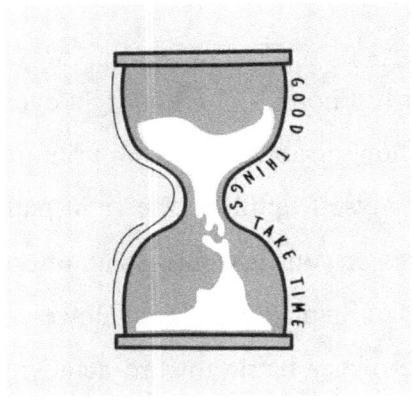

Life has been hard on me, yet I have always made it to my goals, thanks to my learning, skills, and will. Even with the disability, there was no hindrance in my path to success. During the years of my adolescence, I learned that the obstacles in life are inevitable, and this idea is a constant in my world. Whether it is about wrestling with a falling GPA or adapting to vision loss, no, I have learned to overcome them all. I found help promptly when my grades were slipping below average.

The challenges I have faced in my life have given me the courage, motivation, and drive to achieve anything, no matter what life throws at me.

My struggle started with dyslexia, a disease that made me speak, read, and write oddly; it was one of the most painful childhood experiences for me to this day. Being a dyslexic child, I went through a lot, including being bullied at school by other students. For me, dyslexia and her twin sister dyscalculia (a severe difficulty in making arithmetical calculations) made it really difficult for me to give answers to other subjects and to solve mathematical equations. I would just look at the numbers and answer without thinking much about them. I also developed the habit of writing with my left hand, which made things even worse. In my family, working with the left hand was not considered a good practice. Thus, I was discouraged from being a left-handed person; it was even tougher to survive.

Till today, I couldn't tell you the reason why I would just look at the math formulas and give the answers. This was one of the biggest challenges that I had to face in my school years. Because it irritated me when the teacher asked me about how I solved the problem. I simply couldn't explain how I did what I did! As a result, my classmates and sometimes even the teacher would laugh at me. They never understood the fact that I had a condition. It was basically because my brain was moving faster than I could actually solve the problem.

Maybe, this was the reason why I established a hate relationship with math and anything that had to do with numbers. I still wonder if all dyslexia and dyscalculia gave me was a load of frustration and the desire to become the center of ridiculousness. But at the same time, when I look at the brighter side, I realize that it also gave me the power to focus more on reading instead of mathematics.

I was good at writing because I concentrated more on enhancing my vocabulary. Nothing came between me and my passion for studying and acquiring knowledge. Thus, I always got good grades, no matter what. However, I was still struggling in math, and that often upset me a little.

Coping with my condition of dyslexia and dyscalculia was never an easy task for me. I still believe that I would have done better in math if I had been able to do more. But being dyslexic, I had a lot of problems dealing with anything related to numbers. It was difficult to teach myself how to solve an equation. I wanted to ask others for help, but I never wanted them to know about my condition. Therefore, I had to teach myself and do everything on my own.

I did not want others to laugh at me and talk ill about me behind my back. If only they all knew about my condition and my skills with reading, they would never laugh at me. Instead, they would all appreciate me. The major problem was that I knew the answers to all the questions, but I uttered them backward, and nobody understood why. I hid it from everyone because I knew they would laugh. I wanted to face the fact that I didn't have any problem with dyslexia or dyscalculia and that I was dealing with it gallantly. It was actually very frustrating knowing that you could do better, yet you couldn't for fear of criticism. I refused to exert myself beyond my environment and aimed at doing better in life.

Moving forward, I intended to do greater things. So, after finishing high school with a lot of effort, I decided to go into graphic design. I thought that it would allow me to deal with the written work such as printing books, writing papers, working for newspapers, basically, anything that dealt with writing. My passion for writing fascinated me and led me to enter the world of graphic design. I worked wholeheartedly, writing for newspapers and crime agencies.

I soon discovered that I also had an interest in problem-solving activities and unraveling crime cases. So, I enrolled and took the test to work as a corrections officer. I passed the test and eventually worked my way up into the forensic department. My job was to guard criminal cases—finding reasons why they happened. I also took care of the law violating policies and made sure that no one broke the rule, even if it were my own friends. At the same time, I also signed up for the sheriff's office as a correctional officer. I also drove ambulances and did almost anything that could bring me closer to understanding what was going on in our society. I was later offered a job in Miami for the same position. Since it was a good offer, I accepted it promptly.

When I went to the academy for training, I faced some other kinds of challenges because of my being left-handed. I didn't understand which way to go when I was learning to shoot the gun. So, I couldn't make the first cut. Although I learned to shoot with a gun while aiming at the target, I often got confused with which hand I was using. Therefore, it made me take a lot of redos on the shooting range. When I was skilled at shooting, I took the test and secured 48 on 48, which was a record. But being remedial, I didn't get any awards. But then again, it's okay because I knew about my condition and shortcomings.

Nonetheless, all these circumstances didn't get in my way. Nothing possibly demotivated me as I encouraged myself to move forward in my life. Though I had a perfect score after practicing, I couldn't beat it. However, I was content that I passed it with confidence.

The lesson I learned from this incident in my life is that no matter what you are capable of doing, there is no one who can rush you into things. The best part of this learning is that if you want to succeed in any walk of life, you have to educate yourself adequately and consistently.

My challenge of holding a gun with the left or right hand helped me use both hands with perfection. This, as a result, boosted me to get the best scores in the test. Always remember that when you are facing adversity, all you need to do is educate yourself about how to deal with it. Only then can no one stop you and your success.

The teenage years of my life have taught me that whatever life throws at you, deal with it with patience. Just hold on to that belief you have in yourself, and you can do greater things every day. Handle the stress of life with grace, and you'll see how the bad days turn around on you. What I have learned from my struggles through primary and high school is to never depend on anyone for your success. Be diligent enough to teach yourself to face tough times. Be hopeful about the future and never stop struggling.

It is a blessing to be able to rise up every morning and feel the sun on your face. Despite my disabilities, I have trained myself to wake up every morning with a new hope to work harder than yesterday, never allowing anyone to let me down. For me, every day is a new day and another opportunity that others may not have. This life is a gift, and you have to take the opportunity to live it in the best way you can. There are going to be situations when you will find yourself falling into areas that you don't understand. It is up to you to make the best of every situation because no one deserves to ruin or control your life.

There are going to be a number of things that might slow you down. Instead of running away from the challenges, understand that everything happens for a reason; in fact, adversities happen to make you stronger. I know that many times different circumstances in life make you believe that you are not worthy enough, and you become so if you listen to them. So, I need you to know that you should never listen to that voice. Believe that you are worthy, and you really are. You have got this life with a purpose. Sometimes, life can leave you hopeless! But it is you who needs to decide whether you are going to stay helpless on the ground or stand up and make your own path.

You might sometimes find yourself at the end of the rope, and the only thing left for you is to climb up. Instead of making no effort, make sure you take a step. Stop stressing about the days that you cannot control and start focusing on the things that you can do. Take control of your life! Take control of the opportunities! Believe in yourself, and know that it is never over for you. Do not let misery control your life. Do not let anyone tell you how to live your life. Never let anyone validate your purpose or your destiny.

If someone tells you that you are not worthy and are never going to make it, NEVER listen to them. Tell those doubts and excuses in your mind to leave your thoughts. Because this is your life that you are fighting for. Don't wait for something to happen; instead, teach yourself, as I did, how to deal with things that seem hard to do.

Going through the teenage years of my life, where I had to suffer a lot because of my condition, I learned how to refuse to believe the people who judged me. In fact, their dismissal gave me the strength to work harder. I always did what I loved, despite my shortcomings. I have put my interests first because that is what has led me to give my best in whatever field I have been in. However, regardless of the overwhelming odds, I always held that I would find a way.

Chapter 3
Rise Above Life's Sudden Changes

"Be still; quietly remember the presence of and within yourself,
and you will know, without thinking, that while all around you
everything changes, within you lives something unchanging."
-Guy Finley

Just when I thought that things were going fine, and I was settling down with my struggles and shortcomings, in a spur of a moment, everything changed. That's when I realized that life doesn't move in a straight line. The ups and downs keep hitting you time after time. This is reality, and we can never escape it.

In August 2008, I experienced the most crucial change in my life. It was something that turned my world upside down and which tore me apart to my guts. I went from being an average person, regardless of my mental disabilities, to being handicapped for life. This particular incident took almost everything from me, yet I didn't lose hope, which I am thankful for.

I was 29 years old when I got married to this beautiful girl called why (I called her Black Rose). I met her while I was in college, as we were in the same classes. It was love at first sight, and I fell head over heels for her. I remember the first time I saw her; she simply took my breath away. As my eyes followed her as she walked away toward the classroom, she turned around and asked me about the class location mentioned in the orientation map. I was speechless and confused when she asked me that question. Luckily, my friend standing next to me answered her and saved me from coming across as a complete fool. Right when she turned around to leave, she looked back at me and smiled. That was when she stole my heart, and I decided that I would marry her.

Soon, we started seeing each other at college, and our love grew so deep that we decided to get married. After completing college, we got married and moved into the new house that I had bought.

However, before getting married, I had decided not to go back and live on the ranch, so I swore to buy a house for my new family. The day came, and I ended up obtaining a home in Hollywood, Florida. Buying a house was my first investment, and it was a fantastic experience for me. I felt the fullness of a cause for the betterment of my family in the long run. This was the point in my life where I learned that if we make up our minds to achieve something that we really wish for, we will definitely meet it, regardless of the obstacles we face.

This is what I want to tell my readers as well: do not give up and never lose hope that good things will come to you if you just believe. Know that you have the power to become anything you want as long as you are willing to work for it. It is you who has the will and motivation to succeed, because only you can make it happen.

Living in Hollywood, Florida, with my wife, was the life of my dreams. Later, I was blessed with a son who completed our little family. I was living life to the fullest and didn't know that it was short-lived. My most significant gratification in life was that my wife had accepted me with all of my shortcomings, including my disabilities. I thanked God that my son didn't get any of my diseases through inheritance. Life became easy to live as I was happy with everything.

Time went by, and I was transferred to Miami in the same position as a correction officer. While I was working as a correction officer at Miami-Dade Corrections, I encountered a deadly incident. At 33, I almost lost everything I had due to that specific incident. What happened was that an inmate threw some hot liquid at my face, which burned my eyes, and I lost my vision forever. My cornea was burned, and I was unable to see.

It was one beautiful morning. I woke up early to go for a run in a park near my house. Usually, my wife and I used to go together, as we both did cardiac exercises. I tried to wake her up that morning, but she was too tired to get up. It was 6 a.m., and I could hear the birds chirping in my garden with a little bit of sunlight as it was 6 degrees outside. I always liked to go for a jog that early, as it refreshed me and kept me moving for the whole day.

At first, I was not habitually doing exercises in the morning. It was because of my wife, who brought this healthy turnaround in my life. I am thankful to her for that.

Ever since I had started jogging or running or even doing cardio, I started feeling better in my body. It kept me stress-free and energetic for the whole day. This was why I could easily concentrate on my work. As soon as I became used to including physical activities in my daily routine, I couldn't live a day without them because at most times, my body would end up aching. So, this was how I kept myself fit with my healthy daily routine.

Anyways, it was a regular morning that day, and I had not even the slightest idea what was going to happen to me. I came back from a 30-minute run on the beach near my house. By then, my wife had woken up. She knew I was out for a jog, so she started preparing breakfast. As soon as I entered the house, she stood there at the door with a glass of orange juice to welcome me inside. I kissed her and took a sip from the glass, kissed her again because I loved how it tasted, then drank the whole glass in one go.

I then went straight into the shower to clean myself up, got ready for work, and came downstairs. My son was already prepared for school and was there at the breakfast table. My wife had made scrambled eggs with waffles and honey-layered pancakes. I finished my breakfast and left the house with my son to drop him off at school. There were no signs, nor was there any intuition from inside me that something terrible was going to happen that day. Or, maybe if there were, I didn't realize or notice them back then.

At first, when I was near my son's school, I stopped at a signal and started talking to him about his hair looking good. Suddenly a range rover came out ramming in, from the left and was just about to hit me. But luckily, it changed directions at once and broke the signal to pass through. I was jolted for a moment from my chore, but then I thanked God for saving my son and me. The day had just started, and an occurrence like this was a little too much. After dropping my son at the school gate, I turned around my car in the direction toward my workplace.

Suddenly, I felt the need to listen to some good music. I turned on the radio, but there was nothing on it. So, I crouched down to get a CD out of the lower compartment in my car. As soon as I slid down, I didn't notice a heavy truck coming toward me, and I was about to get hit. When I came back up, I saw that massive truck coming right at me while I was still driving. I screamed and at once changed the direction of my car. I was so fortunate to be saved at the very moment, but I still didn't realize that something was always after me. Something wanted to ruin me utterly.

Anyways, I got a lucky stance and escaped death at that time. However, I didn't realize that this was not over and that there was still something in line waiting for me to get caught. I kept driving on the road with fear, as I was still in shock from what just happened. To relax, I stopped at a coffee shop along the way and bought myself a large cup of latte to help me get back to my senses. I took my cup and sat down for a few minutes on a table inside the café. Sitting right there, I kept thinking about what had just happened and why it had happened twice that day. I was freaking out to my core, but I still didn't lose hope.

The next moment, I was driving again in the fastest lane to get to work as soon as possible. As soon as I reached the parking lot outside my office, I stepped out of the car and handed the keys to the valet boy. I moved forward, still having that large latte cup in my hand, toward the security counter. As I leaned down to sign the register at the entrance, I saw a flashing light coming right toward me and shoving into my eyes, leaving them with an extreme burning sensation. I at once lost my sight and couldn't see as my eyes were still closed. By the voices surrounding me as I fell on the ground me, I judged that someone just threw a hazardous hot liquid in my eyes.

People around me were screaming and calling out my name, asking me if I was okay. But unfortunately, I was not. The pain was like a thousand knives being shoved right into my eyes at the same time. I kept rubbing my eyes out of the severe pain, but I noticed someone kept pushing my hands away from my eyes, as it was making things worse. I lay there on the ground for a whole 10 minutes in that unbearable pain until someone put me in the car and took me to the hospital.

Later, I found out that the person who threw the liquid at me was a Hispanic male, and this was all I discovered about him. I didn't even know his name, but I knew that he was an older gentleman. Instead, as I would like to call him, he was a scumbag who threw the hot liquid at me when I was doing my security check at the entrance to my office.

Just when this incident happened, the person with the liquid ran away, leaving behind the bottle he was carrying it in. Instead, all of the other people around had gathered near me to see if I was okay, but I was not. I was in excruciating pain, and nothing helped to calm me down. I was screaming and crying out loud, as I couldn't handle my pain.

I still have no idea why that person did that to me or what his intentions were. However, it did destroy my life in one way or another. Now that I think about that time when I was going through a lot of pain, I realize that I could have died right there. But I survived, and I am still here. I don't know why I was saved, and I am still finding the answer to it. But then, I think that everything in life happens for a reason, which we later realize. That particular moment has now made me stronger than before.

It was the most painful incident of my life, but it also changed my existence as a human being. Time turned everything around, and I became a new person.

Chapter 4
How to Rise Above any Disability

Blindman Walking

"To be blind is not miserable; not to be able to bear blindness, that is miserable."
-John Milton

The next morning, I woke up with swollen eyes that prevented me from seeing anything. For a minute, I thought they were going to explode with that excruciating pain. I was half-blind at the moment since I hit myself against the wall while going to the bathroom. It was tormenting for me since I had no idea that I had gone blind. My blood was gushing through my veins because of the pain and also because of the thoughts shelling my mind that I might not be able to see anymore.

For a moment, everything just stood still. The clock stopped ticking, my brain stopped working, the air around me just froze, my limbs turned motionless, and my conscience halted functioning. Soon, I was haunted by the thought of functioning in the world without sight. How many things will I miss out on while they evolve? What would people think about me? I never wanted to lose my vision, and I had no idea that I was just about to touch the edge of it.

With the help of my inner intuition and since I knew the placement of things in my house and also outside, I somehow managed to reach my car, which was parked on the street. Now that I think about that day, I still have no idea how I got into my car and drove to the hospital. There was something inside of me that was guiding me and telling me what to do next.

I had one of my hands on my eyes to soothe the pain, and with the other, I reached the door of my house. I knew where the car keys were since I had hung them on the key hook bolted to the wall. I touched the wall to find the key hook, and sensing it, I grabbed the car keys, which were hanging on the second hook from the left. After taking the keys, I reached the door, felt the lock, and opened it. There were stairs next to the doormat kept outside. I knew after taking a couple of steps forward, I would reach the first stair. So, moving my left hand around to feel something to hold on to, I, at last, found the staircase to my left.

I held the staircase and took a step forward very carefully to reach the first stair. Just to confirm if it really was the first step of the stairs, I cautiously moved my left foot forward. It was one hell of a job for me to walk like a blind man. I had never thought that I would face something like this in my life. Anyways, as soon as I knew that my first move was successful—stepping on the first stair—I moved my other leg forward to reach for the next step. It was a hedge, having four stairs between the platform and the floor. Thankfully, I stepped down, all of them reaching the ground.

I stumbled badly as I walked toward my car, which was parked across the street. Since I had one hand on my eyes, I was moving my other hand to feel or sense anything that came in my way. Somehow, at that moment, my sixth sense also got enhanced and turned stronger, which helped me make my way to the car. I opened the door and sat inside, turning on the ignition. For a moment, I tried removing my hand from my eyes to see if I could see the road. Just when I tried to open my eyes with an effort, it felt like I had a thousand knives stuck inside them, and the view of the road went blurry.

It was a ten-minutes drive to the hospital from where I lived. Thankfully, the roads were pretty clear at this time, which helped me to drive quite easily. On my way, I could make out the lights from the streetlights, and just when I thought that I may be able to make it to the hospital without any mishaps, I was hit by another car and found myself almost getting hit by another car. I realized that I wasn't driving in a straight line and tried to get back in the lane. Somehow, I managed to drive myself to the hospital.

I reached the Hollywood Memorial Hospital and gave my car to the valet. I went inside with my hands on my eyes since they were hurting and reached the reception, where I told them that I wanted to get my eyes examined. The girl at the reception asked me to sit in the hallway and wait for the doctors to arrive. But she also realized how much pain I was in, so she called in an emergency. The doctors came running after a few minutes to respond to the emergency call, which was mine.

They put me on a stretcher and pulled me toward the ER, where I was to be examined first. On my way to the theater, I was frequently blacking out. My limbs were getting numb with the pain, and my eyes were burning as if there was fire straight from hell inside them. I was unable to cope with the pain by then and was losing my strength. Being on that bed in the hospital, I completely let myself be at the mercy of the doctors. I relied on them entirely to save me from this torture.

I was half-conscious by the time my stretcher reached the ER and could only hear the voices of the doctors and the hospital staff who were examining my eyes. As I lay there in the hospital bed, I was a mixed bag of emotions. A part of me kept thinking about the happy times I had spent with my family. I could see my wife and son with my closed eyes. It all came back to me like a flash of memory as I was thinking about them. At the same time, I was plagued with thoughts of life before me without my vision. Another voice from inside my head said to me that I was already blind and that I would never be able to recover from it. There was undoubtedly a war waging inside my thoughts between my mind and my inner conscience. Something told me that I was going to be just fine as it was only a phase. But something still said to me that I would have to live the rest of my life as a blind man.

On that bed in the hospital, I was thinking about my family and my responsibilities. Thinking about my wife, I kept wondering what she would do if I went blind. Then, I thought about my son and how he would react when he knew that his father couldn't see. I was lashing out, and it felt as if my brain was going to burst.

After the exam, a doctor told me that I had suffered a corneal burn. I was 33 at the time I lost my sight. They told me that no surgery could bring me back my cornea, and I would have to live with that disability forever. I went to a lot of other doctors as well after that and couldn't find the cure. I received several prescriptions, but none of them did anything. As a result of which, I developed a condition known as photophobia and muscular degeneration with pigmentary changes in my eyes. I could not process light because when I tried to face any brightness around me, it would hurt me. Every time there were flashing lights in the atmosphere, I would start having headaches, irritation, and burning sensations in my eyes, and then several extreme changes in mood would occur.

Learning to survive with that pain forever somehow turned me into a bitter person. The damage was significant enough to ruin my life and take everything away from me. My assets for survival were taken away, and I was left with nothing. Not only was I physically damaged, but I was also emotionally destroyed. Every bone in my body screamed out loud to tell me that I wouldn't be able to do anything now. My life was done. I had no idea why God let that happen to me and why He didn't save me.

I still question if this incident was meant to happen. Was I supposed to lose my sight forever and spend the rest of my life as a blind man? I then remind myself of the fact that everything in our lives happens for a reason. Maybe I was meant to get hurt and lose my sight forever to become a lighthouse for other people surviving with disabilities. The only thing they need to have is a driving force to motivate them. That is all it takes to conquer the world. For me, I am still struggling with the things I face each day to reach that level of excellence. And to tell you the truth, the struggle is like a never-ending process that will keep you on your toes with a desire to become something.

I used to be angry most of the time. I couldn't talk to anyone around me. I felt that life was over, as I was unable to see clearly. Everything was dark, and I felt like I was falling into a pit of darkness. There was gloominess everywhere that sucked all the color out of my life. I wanted to scream at the top of my lungs and beg that higher power to give me back my life. I still don't know what actually went wrong and where, since everything was going fine in my life and I was pretty much settled with my family.

Suddenly, something hit me like a thunderbolt and snatched everything away—my wife, my son, my family, my whole shebang. I was a man with nothing. The tables had turned and left me with nothing of my own. I had zero hopes for my upcoming life and thought that nothing was going to be okay again as before.

It was the darkest moment in my life, and it was hard to handle everything. Just when I needed someone to hold me and console me, I was sitting alone and defeated in my own zone. I was unable to fight the pain and was stuck with it forever. All I had to do was learn how to live with that pain. But I wasn't sure what I was going to do with my life. At times, I used to become extremely despaired that I went to the verge of ending my life. Other times I was a bit hopeful and tried to learn to survive.

The times when I wanted to teach myself to accept the pain, I also realized how hard it is to bear it and absorb it inside your soul. I realized how painful it is to actually lose your sight since your eyes allow you to see the world and enable you to use your ability to walk and work with your hands.

For a moment, just try imagining yourself having no ability to see the things around you. Would you be able to take even a single step back or forth? Would you be able to tell who is standing next to you? Would you be able to decide where you want to go? You would only be left with the senses to feel, touch, and think. And that is precisely what I was going through. This became my reality. I was no longer able to judge or determine someone's characteristics by merely looking at them. I instead had to learn to feel things through the sense of smell and the vocal cords. And this, ladies and gentlemen, was not easy at all. In fact, I am still learning day by day and step by step to judge things by their feelings or smells.

I still have to learn to count the steps everywhere I go. I have to touch the walls to know their texture and listen to the sound of the floor to distinguish between a carpeted one and a bare one. I have to rely entirely on my memories to figure out what's coming up in my life. I never knew that I would depend on my recollections of things that I once saw. But I guess it is true what they say. When one of your senses becomes disabled, the other ones get enhanced in an instance. I remember that after the incident, my sense of smell increased immensely. I found that I was able to feel the emotions of the people much more deeply around me. I could tell who they were just by hearing them and feeling their energy instead of judging them by the way they looked.

Having a disability can make even the easiest task of the day the most difficult one. The results can vary with the intensity of pain you have gone through while performing them. It can frustrate you or demotivate you to the extent that you want to give up. But no matter what, you need to keep your calm and emphasize the things that you are doing for now with the thought they will get better in the future. If you put off doing the things that you now find hard to handle, it will only create further problems for you. That is what I have learned from my experiences so far.

After finding out that my cornea was burned so severely that I would never be able to see things clearly again, I became the world's biggest procrastinator. I used to linger on the works that I used to do within minutes previously. Right from there, things started to get worse for me. However, this behavior only caused me more trouble. My life began to turn into a nightmare until I took hold of it. Things began to pile up, be it at home or at work, and everything became messier by the day. This caused me a lot of frustration and agitation, and I went into severe stress and anxiety.

Still, I had one thing on my mind. And that was, that I was to have any hope of getting my life back in order, I was going to have to learn to live with my debility. And for that,

I needed to learn the techniques that would later become my driving force to keep me motivated. I taught myself to keep my cool and not mess around.

By only changing my outlook toward life, I noticed that things were falling into place for me. I learned to confront my anger and my inner feelings of helplessness. This encouraged me to realize that I was my own help and that I had to fix everything around me by myself. This is the optimism that I learned when I started managing things without any help. If you truly believe that you can do what has to be done, it will often give you a push that will make you get started.

Remember, if you are disabled and you need to stand upon your own feet, you will get setbacks and resentments. You will face anxiety when you see your goals crushed. But the only cure for this disease of disparity is to stay positive. This is the only driving force that will keep you motivated in the long run. Nonetheless, never expect things to change overnight. Fuel up your procrastination with the power of positivity and stay motivated.

The struggle to determine what is in my surroundings is still not over. However, being a blind man, I am learning how to be perfect with my disabilities.

Chapter 5
How to Overcome Suicide
A Decision Between Life and Death

*"If a man can bridge the gap between life and death, if he can live
on after he's dead, then maybe he was a great man."*
-James Dean

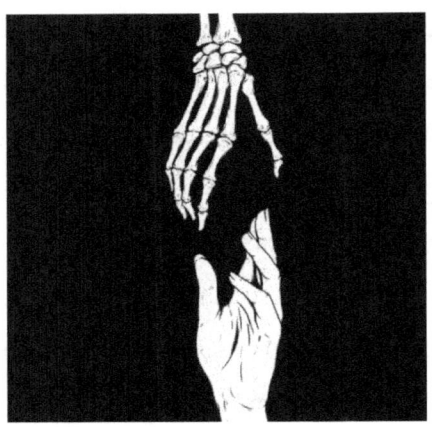

It's sad how your lifelong dream sometimes doesn't
come true. I have an Associates in Art and an Associates in
Science in graphic design, but unfortunately, that ship sank.
It's safe to say I was devastated, and my optimism was

shattered. A while after losing my sight, life began to change drastically. I was left alone on the shore with nowhere to go. Lost, confused and alone, I contemplated taking my own life.

My disability came at a time when I was going through a divorce with my wife of six years, which was something I couldn't afford because our marriage was already hanging by a thread for the last six years. When I lost my sight, we were in the middle of the divorce process, but we were still living in the same house until our divorce was finalized.

Nothing between us was working out, even though we had two sons (my wife did not find that a reason enough to work things out with me). We had differences that never let us coexist peacefully, let alone get along. After a few years of our marriage, we both realized that it wasn't working out and that we should call it quits because we could not preserve the little bit of friendship and love between us for the sake of our children. She had an outlook that was completely different than mine. She even saw the world from the exact perspective to which I objected. It's not that I didn't love her, but I think she never understood me. In fact, she never even tried to understand me.

The worst part of this marriage was that she acted like our marriage was the biggest regret of her life. I never got the love or care that I was entitled to as a husband or significant other. Whenever I needed assistance, she would reluctantly help me. She seemed least interested in my existence. I felt as if she would rather have me dead than live a disabled life.

One day, I was looking for my cane because I wanted to go out for a walk. I asked my wife if she had seen it, but she didn't reply at first, hoping that I'd think that she wasn't around in the room even though I could sense that she was in the same room as me. She was probably busy with her own thing. So, I asked her again, "Honey! Have you seen my crutches?"

She didn't reply again, as if she had completely ignored me. This got really on my nerves, and so after a pause of a few more minutes, I called her out by her name and asked her one more time.

"Greta? Darling? Are you there? Do you know where my white cane (walking stick) is?" she replied annoyingly as if she was least bothered.

"Yeah. It's there by the wall beside the cupboard at your right."

It seemed as if she was telling me to take it myself. But since I couldn't do anything, I stood there for a minute. Thankfully, she soon realized this and got me the stick.

"Thank you, honey," I said to her.

She never replied, and I sensed that she completely ignored me and went back to the sofa where she was sitting and did something that I didn't know. I took my stick and went outside the house to take a walk in the street. I had started wearing dark shades since my eyes were unable to reflect the sunlight. They used to burn whenever I went outdoors during the day.

As I walked down the road with the help of my crutches, I felt torn up inside. Losing my sight made me dependent on someone who couldn't care less about me. I felt awful knowing that my wife didn't want to be there for me when I needed her the most. I fought with the universe and questioned God, asking him why he would let something so terrible happen to me. It was something that I had never imagined. I used to internally fight a new battle for survival every day. I felt inferior and worthless—like I didn't belong. Nothing pleased me except the thought and possibility of regaining my sight.

While I was strolling down the street deep in my thoughts, I kept going through random outbursts of rage. I kept thinking about my future and my present while reminiscing about my past. Tears came streaming down my face. I wiped them off immediately, hoping that nobody around me would notice.

Right there, I felt like a failure—a man who had never achieved anything in life, neither a career nor a family. I took a turn and decided to head back home since I'd been walking for an hour and didn't want to go too far. As I was walking back home, I realized that strangers respected my disability and cared enough to voluntarily help guide me, unlike my wife.

People would come up to me and hold my hand to help me sit in a chair if I wanted to. This made my heart melt for them with gratitude. Others would help me climb down the stairs of the Metrorail that led to my house. And I would appreciate their help with all of my heart. At that time, I realized that there are good and bad people everywhere. It's just a matter of getting along with the good ones while keeping a distance from the malevolent ones, for they would sap all your energy with their negative vibes.

That day, when I reached home, I heard thrashing noises coming from upstairs. I called my wife to check if she was okay.

"Darling? You okay, honey?"

One of my sons ran downstairs to me, held my hand, and led me upstairs to the bedroom where my wife was. I kept asking him what was wrong and if everything was okay. But he didn't even say a word.

I asked him again, angrily, "Mike? Come on! Tell me what's wrong with your mum? What are these thudding noises that I can hear? What's going on?"

I was afraid to find out if something had happened to my wife. Since I couldn't see anything, I feared handling things on my own. I felt like I was good for nothing and that I was helpless when it came to helping others. Mike took me to the room, opened the door, and let me in. I could still hear those pounding thuds and knew that she was there.

I asked her again, "Greta, darling. What's going on? Are you throwing things away? Are you okay?"

From her panting breath, I could already sense that she was feeling some kind of discomfort and was up to something. I understood from her tone that she was angry. Right after hearing my voice, I heard her burst out in a loud cry. She started weeping then and there, as if she were frustrated. I went closer to her to pat her back and asked what was wrong with her. As soon as I put my hand on her back, she pushed it away.

"This is enough. This is not what I signed up for! I'm gonna leave now. I can't be around a sick man who is not able to do his own stuff," she burst out furiously.

"Oh, and by the way, would you like to tell me how long this is gonna last? Are going to be a mean person? I mean, will you keep relying on other people's help all your life? There are a ton of disabled people out there who are living by themselves without the help of others. And look at you," she said, being extremely sarcastic.

I was standing right there, listening to her brash voice in anger as she recalled several of my inevitable shortcomings. I felt so weak at that moment, and I just wanted to end my life at that very moment. But I stood there in front of her with my head down while I fought to hold back my tears.

"I have never stopped you. You are free to leave if you want. I know that our marriage is dying, and we are on the verge of a divorce. It is just for our kids that we are still together under the same roof, where you are bearing all of my inadequacies. But I won't stop you now. You can leave right now even before the divorce gets finalized," I spoke in a lower voice than hers, calmly.

That was the moment where things ended between my wife and I. I let her go forever, and that was how she left me. She wasn't too fond of me before I lost my sight. But when I became disabled, she couldn't even stand me. And so there was no point in us staying together, even if it was just for the sake of our kids. However, there was one thing that's still true. The reason I let her go was that I wanted her to be happy since I loved her.

She left with both of my sons as the divorce got finalized a couple of months later. After the annulment of our marriage, the state took my kids into official custody. This happened because my ex-wife had made a false statement to kill herself and my sons. That was one of the toughest times in my life, knowing that my children were away from me—in the custody of strangers.

I decided to keep my sons with my brother and his wife. The reason why I chose my brother and his wife to be the caretakers of my children was that my brother's wife was my ex-wife's sister. Therefore, I found them both to be the most reliable sources in this regard. Nonetheless, it was also easily accessible for both of us parents to communicate with our children despite our own differences.

After the divorce, I was sitting down one day in my living room, thinking about the things I had lost. For a moment, I felt completely numb. I was comparing my past with my present and analyzing my future. I realized that even though I had dyslexia in my childhood, I was able to acquire the best somehow. This gave me hope for my future, thinking that if my downsides didn't stop me from achieving my goals in the past, there was no reason for them to stop me now.

But suddenly, something took over me again. It was another panic attack accompanied by severe anxiety, stress, and depression that quickly conquered my soul. I was in an extremely vulnerable state, both physically and emotionally. I couldn't decide what to choose. Life or death? I didn't know where to go or who to ask for help.

I was filled with anger and had an urge to avenge my failures. I couldn't smile even if I wanted to. Neither could I feel anyone else's happiness. My appetite was gone, and I barely ate. As a result, my weight dropped drastically. I was angry at the world because it seemed like a dark place to live, with no happiness or hope around. I didn't want people to feel sorry for me—I didn't want their pity. In fact, all I wanted to do was figure a way out of this.

I didn't look forward to the future because my life seemed like a dark tunnel with no light to be found. I was utterly lost and regretted my existence. I knew I was falling right into the pit of depression since it was sucking my soul out. I knew how things worked in this situation since I was going through the same thing. I was indecisive about my life and choices. I had no idea what to do—to live or to die. I was battling with the thoughts of either living as a disabled person or giving up once and for all.

Then came a night in my messed-up world, and suddenly, everything changed. I felt a ray of sunshine, and I was hopeful again, and there came a desire to live a life full of dreams and aspirations. One night, while I was sitting despondently in my room, something aired on the TV that caught my attention. I heard the news about David Patterson, who was a visually impaired person, being appointed as the governor of New York. The news hit me like a giant rock, but this time, it was a good feeling. It was one of the pivotal moments in history when a blind man was appointed as the governor of a state like New York.

This was my moment! This was the moment where I chose life over death. I heard the news on TV, and I was stunned, thinking about how a man who cannot see can run errands and possess great authority. I was inspired by his courage and fearlessness to attain his goals, including becoming governor. Whereas, I lay there in my house, brokenhearted and empty-handed. This inspiration encouraged me to stand up from the ground again, lifting my hopes, and to live life to the fullest despite my disability. Now, when I look back at that very moment, I feel content about choosing life instead of death. I know that I made the right decision to live and not to give up during one of my darkest hours.

I got up and shook off my disparity with the motivation to live my life in my own way. I started searching for places that teach visually impaired people to become independent. I found the Lighthouse of Broward, a nonprofit organization that helps the blind and visually impaired become independent. That was the time when I decided to go to school and learn independent living skills. These skills included instructions about how to type on a computer without being able to see or read through a specific software program called JAWS. I had lost my vision, but I did not lose my mind. My wits were still in the right places, and I was in a much better state to start studying again after everything that I'd gone through.

Meanwhile, the state of Florida offered the "Bureau of Business Enterprises (BBE)" program for the visually impaired to run businesses on their own. I got enrolled without any delays and soon acquired the certifications. I was never afraid to learn, and that is why I also have the desire to teach others to rise above everything, against all odds. I completely denied my infirmities, which is how I was able to turn the negative things into positive ones by facing my fears. My upsurge was an answer to all those who considered the accident "the fall of mighty Gary."

Chapter 6
Become the Most Powerful
Person Alive
What Comes After the Blues

"If you feel lost, disappointed, hesitant, or weak, return to yourself, to who you are, here and now and when you get there, you will discover yourself, like a lotus flower in full bloom, even in a muddy pond, beautiful and strong."
-Masaru Emoto

Hundreds of years ago, Alexander Graham Bell made an optimistic statement that changed my life forever. He said, "When one door closes, another opens." This proved to be true for me. In my opinion, if fate had taken away my sight, it didn't matter, because it couldn't take away my courage or my strength to move on.

I had nothing to lose in my life because everything that I could call mine was gone. My house, the cars, my family, my job—nothing remained. I was left with no hope for tomorrow, and I felt as if darkness had taken over. I was drowning in an ocean of sorrow and despair, but then came the most pivotal moment in my life, and everything changed.

I rented my friend Bretman's studio apartment. I was very appreciative of the fact that he'd always been too generous and kind toward me. He helped me with all the arrangements I needed. He supported me in all sorts of ways and helped raise my spirits until I found a job to get back on my feet. I would always be grateful for his help, support, and trust.

After everything I had gone through because of my bad decisions, he never criticized me for any of my wrong choices or shortcomings. He always made sure and tried his best to make me feel happy, even on my darkest days. He would help out with whatever I needed. He taught me how to walk with crutches, even though I was still married to my wife back then, and she never bothered helping.

Anyway, never mind. Bretman brought breakfast for me every morning until I learned how to cook for myself. He even went out of his way and ordered lunch for me every day from his office. And then at night, he would bring food for us on his way home from work, or we'd make dinner together. Bretman proved to be a great friend—he never let me miss a meal the entire time I was with him.

Even in my unhappiest hours, as I battled depression and anxiety, Bretman would always pump me up with motivational thoughts. He told me to rid my mind of all negative and suicidal thoughts. He'd always encourage me by telling me that it's just a phase and that, in time, I'd make peace with my reality and get used to living a different lifestyle with disabilities. He reassured me that one day I would stand up on my feet again and beat the odds by living the life I'd always imagined.

My best friend tried every possible way to keep me motivated and constantly kept encouraging me to not give up. But I still didn't know what kept pulling me back somehow. I felt a force behind me, like human hands hauling me through my waist into a deep and shady ditch. It felt as if this thing didn't want me to get up or get better. When Bretman would talk to me, I would feel much better, but only for the moment.

His pep talk was only helpful in his presence; after he'd leave, I'd go back to feeling the way I did before. That eerie murky cloud of pessimism took over me again, and I could literally hear voices in my head—I thought I was hallucinating. The voices in my head kept whispering things in an attempt to make me give up. They'd say that I was a dead man and nothing will ever be the same again. They told me I was never going to live a respectable life again.

Sometimes, I'd shut them out. But other times, they would conquer it all, shadowing my entire being with those sullen, shabby, boney hands, luring me into a mysterious pit, driving me to the irresistible urge of killing myself. Whenever I attended to those voices and did what they asked, like holding a gun to my head or holding a knife to my throat, waiting to slit it open, I could literally hear the sardonic laughter, as if those voices were pleased by my actions.

One time, I was lying on my bed; I don't exactly remember what time of day it was since it all seemed the same to me—nothing mattered. I looked up at the roof with my shades on. My eyes were stoned, and my lashes didn't blink for long. My brain was running swiftly with the thoughts of hanging between life and death.

All those feelings, paired with the sounds inside my head, kept colliding. I got up from bed, stiff and straight like a cold dead body, and went upstairs, straight to the kitchen. It was like something was guiding me which way to go. I had no idea what was happening to me at that moment.

As soon as I reached the kitchen cabinet, I opened the second drawer with all the cutlery in it. I reached out for the biggest knife, gripped it tight, and took it. I closed the drawer and, with the knife in my hand, headed toward the living room. I stood right there in front of the glass window. The voices in my head kept telling me to finish it off once and for all because I had no reason to live.

As soon as I put the knife to my throat, the door opened, and someone entered. It was Bretman. She was the only one who had spare keys to my apartment for my convenience and safety (thank God). As soon as she got in, she called out my name twice, but I didn't answer. The window where I was standing was at the extreme left corner from the entrance, which is why she couldn't see me from the front door.

As she moved a couple of steps forward and looked around, she found me on the left side of the house, in front of the big glass window. She called out to me from behind,

"Gary? Baby? What are you doing here, standing in front of the window?"

As she moved closer, she saw me holding a knife to my throat and immediately jumped up and snatched the knife from my hand.

"What are you doing, man!? Are you crazy? Why are you doing this?"

She threw the knife away and held me tight. She burst into tears as he embraced me. It felt like a genuine brotherly hug from the truest person in my life who sincerely cared about me. Before that day, my faith in humanity had shattered and fallen apart. There were people in my life who had broken my trust many times, because of which I had a hard time trusting people. I was left with nothing at all. I had developed trust issues with people around me, which made my life even more miserable. But after Bretman saved my life, my confidence in mortality was restored.

His sincerity for me touched me, and I couldn't help but weep like a baby. The feelings I had at that very moment were indescribable. It was like a balloon full of sadness and remorse had suddenly burst to let everything out. In that particular moment, I cried a river. I even screamed out, as if I were crying over my disabilities and shortcomings. A lot was going on in my life that I didn't know how to process.

The rock that was building up inside of me because of all the negativity had suddenly disappeared, thanks to one person.

It was Bretman's shoulder that I cried on. He was there to console me all the time, no matter what, and to always motivate me. All I still remember about that night is that it was both the most atrocious and the most rampant. It was the night I decided that I would do something for myself and would never listen to the voices in my head again. Those feelings were slowly killing me, and I couldn't afford to feel that bad ever again.

But deep down, I knew it wasn't an easy task to get over those suicidal thoughts. As per the voices inside my head, it was only the first attempt, and they wouldn't let go of me that easily. However, what I learned from that night was that I was alone in that fight. And I had to drag myself out of that dusky pit of hopelessness and death.

After that first encounter with bereavement, the more I tried to get over those feelings, the more they overcame me. I was constantly fighting with my inner self to stand my ground and not give in this time around. But being the weak human being that I was, I used to fall prey to them and give in, unfortunately.

At the first time of my deadly encounter, I was saved by fate in the shape of my best friend. It was the second time now, and I noticed being lured toward death valley. Another fine day, when I was alone in my house, I started hearing the voices again, which led me straight to the glass window again. Something inside me drove me to open the window. Since I was living on the 17th floor, the air pressure was quite high. The lightest blow could make anything disappear in the blink of an eye, due to the strong winds. I was standing at the edge of the window sill, on the verge of ending my life with just one jump.

It's like I was hypnotized and couldn't hear a single noise in the background, but suddenly my phone rang, and I got distracted for a minute. I was literally saved by the bell! Shaking my head in disappointment and fear, I promptly blinked three times or maybe more so I could come back to my senses. It felt as if I'd been sleepwalking, and then suddenly, the phone rang and brought me back to reality. I wondered where I was standing since I felt the massive air pressure on my body. As soon as I looked at my feet standing at the height of 17 stories, I let out an incoherent mumble and immediately stepped back.

I was scared to death as I realized what would've happened had I not come back to my senses. My eyes were filled with tears, and my mouth was as dry as a desert. But the phone kept ringing in the background. I looked around in confusion, as I didn't know what to do. My eyes were looking for my phone in the room since I couldn't find it. After a minuscule search, I found it on the couch. I answered the call, and yet again it was Bretman, my saving grace.

"Oh, boy! You saved my life again, man!" The words came out of my mouth involuntarily as soon as I heard his voice on the other end.

It wasn't too soon, as darkness kept following me everywhere. I was still stuck in the cave of depression and anxiety. Despite my friend's encouraging words, I still used to have episodes of severe depression where I'd get the constant urge to end my life. However, I still managed to fight the pessimistic rock inside me and crush it into pieces.

Then, finally, one night, every cynical feeling came to an end. At last, I discovered a way for the voices to leave my mind and body when I decided to end the struggle and started acting on them. I was home one night thinking about the miseries I had endured, and I remember craving a cup of coffee out of nowhere. I got up and, surprisingly, didn't feel the need to hold my crutches. I went to the kitchen and made myself a cup of coffee, and came back to the lounge, where the TV was already on. I grabbed the remote and kept switching the channels, looking for something good to watch.

Luckily, I stopped at one channel where the news about a blind politician was being aired. The newscaster told us that David Patterson, a visually impaired politician, was elected as the governor of New York. This piece of news proved to be a turning point for me. It was at that moment that I decided to let go of all my fears and start living life on my own without relying on anyone's help.

I realized that life didn't end just because I had lost my eyesight and that there was a long way to go for me. I held my hopes up high and hung on to dear life to support me in my future endeavors as I laid the foundation of self-confidence by believing in myself to live a healthy life. The inspiration I got from David Patterson made me realize that it doesn't matter what your disabilities are or what race you belong to; you can be destined for greatness even after your fall. That moment, I realized that the best was yet to come.

Despite his blindness, nothing stopped David Patterson from becoming the governor of New York. This was what inspired me the most: his enthusiasm and his spirit of never giving up on his dreams. I thought about how well I actually knew myself. The inner-me answered that I had a passion for reading, elevating myself, and inspiring others. I believed in my call from the heavens to get back on my feet again. That moment felt like all the trumpets were being blown for me as the doors to heaven opened. As a reply to the heavenly call, I positively honored the opportunity and said yes to myself to be anything that I wanted to be.

I believed that my disability would no longer define me. The only thing I had to focus on was to make myself available for everything life had in store for me and to become a better person, irrespective of my disability. The moment when David Patterson came on TV as the governor of New York was like a wake-up call for me. It was the thunder that roamed across the sky. That day I told myself that despite being visually impaired, I still have ears to listen to, hands and legs to move, and a fully functioning brain to work my way around daily life.

I learned from life that just when you are about to give up, your life can turn around drastically. I learned how to stop wishing and start doing what I wanted. It was time for me to take action to achieve my goals. The harsh realities of life taught me that the willingness to rebuild yourself can change darkness into light. Even though I had no hopes for tomorrow, I knew that my abilities to learn, read, and elevate myself above all odds were the only things that held my head up.

So, I decided to educate myself on how to create a better tomorrow for myself and eventually for my sons as well. I sold my Glock 17 and started searching for a blind school. I found one called the Blind Lighthouse of Broward, where I soon registered myself and waited to hear back from them. I got a home visit from one of the counselors who came to check if I was really a visually impaired person and was eligible to get enrolled in their school. They checked all of my documents and invited me to join the school as soon as possible.

After my return to normal life, I realized that nothing was over. I still had a chance to push myself to the limits of my success. I knew that the sun would shine again.

This is why I urge everyone going through testing times to never give up and learn from their experiences. Believe that the sun will shine again—brighter than before. But remember, this can only happen when you allow it to shine on you. And then, when you feel the sun on your skin, it doesn't matter how bright it is; you will still feel the warmth and light sweep away the darkness inside you, and that will be enough.

Chapter 7

How to Shine Above Darkness

"Just as despair can come to one only from other human beings, hope, too, can be given to one only by other human beings."
-Elie Wiesel

I became hopeless after losing my sight. I had a feeling that my accident wasn't fate; it was intentional—a conspiracy of some sort. And because of it, I was stuck in a miserable life. If there was hopelessness in my life because of someone, there was also hope because of someone, just as the quote by Elie Wiesel states.

I used to think that I was more unfortunate than others. I thought recovery was as impossible as saving the world. People with depression usually think less about their future because, to them, it is not something worth counting on or looking forward to. The same happened to me as well. I had lost all hope for a good future. Such situations come as no surprise to those who are going through the same. Because depression is something that completely changes your perspective on life, it becomes quite painful to imagine the opportunities lying ahead in your future. I came to know about a psychiatrist, Bessel van Der Kolk, who stated that healthy people can imagine almost everything about their future in random patterns.

The trauma that I had experienced led me to believe that there wasn't a way out. The only thought that persistently took over my mind was to end my life.

Depression never let me make it through the day without feeling like I was completely hopeless and done for. I couldn't get through a task as simple as getting out of bed in the morning because that's how miserable I had become.

Then, suddenly, one day, it all went away. That day, I realized that depression always misleads. Standing at the bay of my severe depression and anxiety, I found the encouragement and motivation to live again with the help of a blind politician who appeared like a ray of hope for me.

I understood that the same muscles that are used to survive depression and anxiety are the same muscles that help resist the dark wave of hopelessness. Yes, ladies and gentlemen, it all comes down to hope.

Hope is not merely about positive thoughts or living in a utopian world or a fantasy. "Hope" means to stay dedicated and work toward the concept of life even when you see darkness at the end of the tunnel. Hope is a force to be reckoned with; it is the strength that keeps you moving. It hurts the most initially, but as you get used to the pain and become stronger, everything becomes easier as you progress gradually.

Hope makes everything possible. It is not easy to think about the nearly impossible things that could ever occur. But I know that it does work out in the end, eventually. Hope is not an attitude; it is an act. It is acting as if there might be a future, even when the situation indicates otherwise.

You are already aware of all the scary times that I went through when I wanted to take my own life. I was lucky enough to have the support of a very dear friend of mine, who dragged me out of the pits of despair. Categorically, nothing was ever tougher in my life than coming back from those dumps. I got a chance to learn how to subsist on my own by flouting the exceedingly shrewd voices in my head. These voices advised me to give up and convinced me that it was the easier thing to do. I had accepted that recovering from this condition was not for me and that I had to fight it all of my life if I stayed alive.

In times of disparity, you survive through thick and thin because you realize that your life matters as much as anyone else's. When the world mocks you and tells you that you are worthless of sympathy because of what and who you are, being kind to yourself is an act of revolt.

Some of you would rather give in because it all seems exhausting and scary at first. And some of you would slightly tuck yourselves under the cozy blanket of the comforting lies of depression. But I wasn't a coward, and I know that neither are you.

The first step after overcoming depression and stepping into a new world of hope was going back to school. It wasn't easy since it required twice the struggle. I decided to do my bachelor's in criminology. I also got my license for running a vending machine business.

But first, I wanted to complete my degree because that was the plan even before I lost my sight. The worst part of going back to school and studying was that many people discouraged me because of various factors. They told me that I would never be able to achieve what I wanted. There was again this loop of deterrence and doubts in the way of proving myself. But until then, I had momentarily learned how to unfold the barriers and untie the knots that stopped me from doing the things I wanted to do.

The very first week of school was a bit challenging for me. None of my classmates were ready to welcome a blind student. As soon as I entered the classroom, they used to look at me surprisingly, as if some alien had entered the room. Secondly, I was the oldest one among all the other students. How would it be for a 40 years old man to study with students younger than him? It was strange and tough to handle, too, because sometimes I also felt embarrassed being among people with such a significant age gap.

I was unable to read from the textbooks, which was a challenge for me. But what was more intriguing and difficult for me was to compete against younger students. I had to rely on someone on days when PowerPoint presentations were going on. I had to ask one of the students to explain them to me due to my inability to see.

Being the only blind person listening to the professor's lecture and having to do homework without sight was an unusual thing for me. It was not an easy task. I was struggling, but I didn't lose hope. Nothing stopped me, even when my grades in the first semester didn't turn out as I expected. Yet, I worked harder and pushed myself to achieve what I set out to accomplish.

As a result, my grades started to improve by the second semester. I also started to feel comfortable in the classroom. What was more challenging for me was that I couldn't see what the professor was writing on the board. They showed pictures and played movies that I was unable to watch. I used to analyze those movies and conclude what they were about based on their audio.

Therefore, I sometimes felt annoyed and even got mad at myself since I could not tell what was going on. Yet, I worked hard and didn't let this irritability get to me.

I courageously went to class and asked questions enthusiastically. I asked for help as well, and thankfully some students helped me out. They helped me take notes and provided all the details. They would also volunteer to help me out at school with different tasks. I was lucky in this regard to have the support of my classmates despite my disability. Without them, I don't think I would have been able to make it. I felt blessed.

I knew, at first, that it would be hard. But when I decided not to give up and remained determined, the doors started opening for me. I pushed myself through it and finally achieved my goal. Quitting is never the solution to the hard times that you face. Instead, sticking to your plan always makes a difference. And the rewards you get in the end are worth the struggle.

I used to miss the bus to school, and since I couldn't drive, it was sometimes difficult for me to reach school on time. I knew that this was another challenge for me. Therefore, I didn't stop there and turned back, giving up on myself. I kept on thriving until I achieved what I desired, just as I had planned.

Living alone was another challenge for me. And going to school and running the vending machine business at the same time was a lot for me to handle. Making sure that everything was in its place and working smoothly was a tough job. I didn't know how I would be able to manage these things on my own. But when I had faith in myself, everything fell into place.

I don't believe in giving up because quitters never win and winners never quit. What would you do when you realized that you were walking on a rocky road with hurdles leading up to your destination? Would you turn around and go back when the going gets tough or choose to keep walking, overcoming those obstacles courageously? Pursuing your dreams is like running in a marathon, in which the last 3 miles are the hardest. But you know what's lying there at the end of the race if you just push through? It's victory. This is precisely what I did when I pursued my dream of graduating. I never gave up despite the struggle and kept running toward my goal. In the end, I stood victorious.

Although I was visually impaired, I still competed with healthy people and won second place in the department of arts and sciences. For me, it was like winning first place because my struggles were as real as those of normal people. So, it was something exceptional for me to achieve.

At the age of 41, in May 2016, I graduated with a bachelor's degree in criminology; it was an excellent gift to myself. I also received an award for the best undergrad researcher and was later given the opportunity to narrate at the research symposium for disabled students. This was one of the greatest moments of my life, and I felt proud of myself.

I wanted to inspire people around me, and so I did. There were hurdles in my way to success, nonetheless, but they didn't stop me from continuing my endeavor to get my master's degree. I was successful and moved on to achieve my Ph.D.

Albert Einstein once said, "Learn from yesterday, live for today, and hope for tomorrow. The important thing is not to stop questioning."

Chapter 8
How to Transform Impossible to Possible

"Virtually nothing is impossible in this world if you just put your mind to it and maintain a positive attitude."
-Lou Holtz

We all wish for something better than what we think of, which we call our dream. We dream of a good job, a nice house, a settled life, and a secure future, all while dealing with the occasional crisis. These problems can seem to be everlasting, and we hope that they will eventually come to an end. But how do we completely get rid of them? Only if we work hard enough to do so.

We may be trying to make amends in our relationships, trying to rid ourselves of an addiction, or planning to make important career decisions. But, sometimes, even after putting in a lot of effort, we still don't get the results we were expecting. We notice that it has been days, weeks, and months, but not a single thing has improved.

Unfortunately, in such times, it's easy to be discouraged by the current situations you've been dealing with, which eventually compels you to lose hope. You start to think that "this is never going to happen" or "I will learn to live with it." We know that pain is a significant part of life. However, what we don't realize is that this pain is also capable of changing us by teaching us from experience. Heartaches, losses, and disappointments change who we are. Every painful period is emergent.

Eventually, the bad times will pass. But, when you get through it, you will notice a change in yourself. You'll learn that the tough times taught you a valuable lesson while you endured a loss or an illness, and you might let it overwhelm you.

However, remember how the pain changes you; it is entirely up to you since you can either turn out bitter or better. You might end up quitting your passion, or you can come out with a new you and discover a new fire within you to achieve your goals. You can end up hopeless or excited about the array of opportunities in front of you. You can become a whiner or a warrior who knows how to resist all the resentment that gets in the way of reaching your goals. Do not complain about the pain because, without the pain, we wouldn't be able to reach the fullness of our destinies.

Sometimes, we inflict pain upon ourselves by making poor choices and bad decisions, such as proactively ending a relationship just because we thought it wasn't working out. But it becomes painful when it comes to dealing with the consequences. All of us go through some kind of pain. But the real challenge that comes with it is for us not just to go through it but to grow through it. We need to look at the experience as an opportunity for you to get tougher, develop your character, and gain confidence.

People can tear down your spirit by telling you that you're not capable of reaching your goals. But those words do nothing but exhaust you. The pain isn't meant to stop you. It's there to prepare you, cultivate you, and shape you into your ideal.

Difficulties are a part of life; you cannot escape them. So stop telling yourself that you cannot do it. Don't consider yourself weak or powerless. Eventually, the pain will pass, and you will gain new strength. Just because it hasn't happened yet doesn't mean that it's not going to happen at all.

There will always be forces trying to convince us to settle where we are. Life has a way of pushing our dreams down. They tend to be buried under discouragement, past mistakes, divorce, or low self-esteem. Therefore, you need to stop recalling the hurt and pain that you went through. Let it all go, and turn it around by focusing on your dream.

Have you allowed any of your dreams to get buried inside of you? At one time, you believed you were destined for greatness. You believed you could excel in your career. You believed you could break an addiction. But you soon realized that you could not do it. Instead, you had several breakdowns. During such times, you must constantly remind yourself that none of this is your fault.

It's easy to give up and accept a mediocre life, and nobody would fall for you. The enemy would love to deceive you into burying your dream and making you think that it is never going to work out. But never believe those lies. No point in time is ever too late to reach your goals.

Every time you think about your dream, you are removing the dirt and digging it out. The true sign of a champion is that, even if some dirt gets thrown on you, instead of letting it bury you, you keep shaking it off and keep moving forward.

You wouldn't have that opposition if you didn't have something great in you. If your dream wasn't alive and on track, you wouldn't have so many distractions. That dream is still alive inside of you. You may have tried a year ago or 40 years ago. But then you realized that nothing worked out and no one even helped you. Do not get discouraged. Go back and try again. This is your time to shine; this is your moment. Remember that your destiny is calling out to you, and you must answer.

Your dream isn't dead. It's just temporarily out of reach. But remember that your time *is* coming. Good things are coming your way. Possibilities that you have been waiting on and dreams that you have been praying for are on their way.

Average is not your destiny. Constantly struggling and barely getting by is not your story. These minor afflictions are temporary, as are the adversities. But the glory is eternal. You will feel your destiny calling out to you like fire.

You might not have been successful at first, and there must have been times in your life when the loan didn't get approved, you didn't get chosen for the part you wanted to play, or even your medical report didn't turn out well. Remember that it's okay. You still have it in you. Shake off the doubt and the negativity and believe that you are in the right place and time. All you have to do is get into the right frame of mind to accomplish what you've been longing for.

Tell yourself that this is *your* year to get healthy, meet the people you wish to meet, excel in your career, and move toward your ultimate destiny. Keep telling yourself that now is the time to achieve your goals and wishes to break free from this despair and that you will experience happiness. This is your time for restoration, vindication, and new beginnings.

It's easy to settle for mediocrity, but you need to make sure you're headed in the right direction.

As for the story of my life, I'd like to tell you that nothing ever stopped me from achieving my goals. Even though I had been down in the dumps and was on the verge of taking my own life, I didn't quit. Something inside me always kept me going, and that was my faith. I knew that I could do it despite all the negativity around me.

After going back to school and achieving my degree in criminology, I moved on to my next mission, which was to pursue a law degree. My main objective for achieving the law degree was to give back to the community by implementing changes to the existing laws. I wanted to become the voice of disabled people nationwide. I always loved to research the causes of our social issues. For instance, when I participated in an undergraduate research symposium contest, I wrote about disabled students pursuing higher education. I learned that even though the Americans with Disabilities Act (ADA) guarantees the disabled students an even playing field when it comes to training, those services are not always in place. It takes a few weeks, if not months, for an individual to gain proper help from the institution.

I think that all these institutions need to be ready for members of the disabled community as well, since they are mostly for non-disabled or normal participants. I noticed that disabled people face similar struggles in the criminal justice system. So, after becoming a lawyer, I decided to work with organizations to help promote inclusion for people who have an impairment.

As a young man, I could not distinguish between situations where I should or should not adapt based on the ways things were changing around me. I have come to understand the fundamental differences between adaptation and overcoming. I've chosen to make the best of what life throws at me. I have learned from all the changes I went through. I learned that it is not the hurdles; instead, it is how we deal with them. As a result of the hardship, I discovered that I seem to perform best under pressure and challenges.

Just because you're unable to do something doesn't mean it's impossible for you to do so. Today, the world has made almost everything possible. Technology has taken over, and we have plenty of resources at the tip of our fingers. Things around us might be difficult, but that doesn't mean we should give up.

So, if there's nothing in this world that's impossible, there's no harm in wishing for what seems impossible. It is necessary to know that not everyone will accompany you in following your dream and that not everyone will agree with your decisions. People won't have the same perspective as you.

You need to know that you're the only one who can do it. You need to believe and have faith in your dreams and vision. You ought to know that even if no one else sees it for you, you must see it for yourself.

If you wish to be the best and reach the pinnacle of success, then know that there is no way around it. You *must* be focused on your goals at all times. For greatness can never be achieved without passion. If you want to make your dreams come true, then you must associate yourself with champions.

Chapter 9
How to Find your Hand of Pearls

"Nothing stops the man who desires to achieve. Every obstacle is simply a course to develop his achievement muscle. It's a strengthening of his powers of accomplishment."
-Thomas Carlyle

It is not easy for a disabled person to live a normal life. Yet, if they have the will, they are capable of conquering mountains. This was exactly what I did in my days when I wanted to achieve something in life. I never wanted to be an embarrassment—neither for myself nor for society. I wanted to do something that would encourage not only the disabled but normal people as well to strive harder toward achieving their goals.

Life is unpredictable because you never know what will happen next. Yet, in whatever state we are in, we need to plan out our lives to become secure in every aspect. You might not know what the future brings. You might not know whether your plans will work out for you or not. But still, you need to keep your spirits high by believing in yourself. And then one fine day you will notice that you got it all, just by keeping your hopes up.

Although my life has been a trail of odds and challenges, even then, despite my incapacity to see, I trained myself to live a normal life with normal people. Regardless of all the discouragements I received, I never lost hope and stopped believing in myself, which is why my struggles paid off well.

I received a second-place award for research regarding the lives of disabled students in higher education. It wasn't an easy task for me as I went through a lot of difficulties. Yet I learned that hard work never goes to waste. And so the next award that I achieved was for outstanding undergraduate research. Each department nominated their best student, so I was selected by the department of arts and sciences to receive the award.

My next big achievement was making the front page of the Sarasota Herald Tribune for being entitled to the hard-won master's degree as a blind man. I was more than glad about my accomplishment, but sadly, I couldn't read the text of the news.

Next in line was the achievement of the state acquiring the vending machine business. The vending machine business is a program that is provided through the state of Florida. There is a bill called the Randolph-Shephard Act that allows the visually impaired to operate a business. Usually, the visually impaired people used to sell pencils and papers at the courthouse. But now, thanks to the Randolph-Shephard Act, disabled people are enabled to run a cafeteria, a snack bar, or a vending route. Generally, the vending route was for people who had been in the program for the longest time.

When I was studying at the lighthouse school for the blind, I had the option of learning how to have a regular job or start a small business. But there was no knowledge of that. However, I searched and learned that the state of Florida, in fact, does provide a program where the visually impaired are enabled to run small businesses. But to enroll in that program, you'll have to pass all the tests at the school once every six months. Even if they passed the test and qualified for it, the jobs or businesses were not guaranteed for them.

However, in 2011, I took all the classes and applied for the certification of food-service manager to run a business. I also passed the state exam to acquire my license from the state. When all of my documentation was cleared, I was finally qualified to run a business. From that day onward, my life was changed forever, as I had accomplished things as an independent entrepreneur.

The vending machine business is a part of the food industry. My work is to fill up the snack-making machines with frozen food and drinks, making sure that people are well fed in order to imply customer satisfaction rules.

If you have the will to do something, don't think about how hard it is going to be. Don't think about the questions or the headaches involved. I had to jump through a lot of hoops to get what I wanted because I had always resisted the idea that my disability would sweep me to the sidelines of life.

Up until now, I have struggled very hard to establish myself as an entrepreneur. And so, moving on, I want others to take notes from my story, as I want to help others overcome the obstacles in their lives. I thrive on helping people with special challenges live active and purposeful lives. I want them to know that what is within them is bigger than what is in their path to success, and that is their will to stand firm.

Know that life is a struggle, a challenge, and suffering. It is not always rainbows and butterflies; it is the compromise that moves us along. Whenever you strive for something, you are not going to win every time. Instead, you are going to go through setbacks and failures. You might see your dreams failing and your hopes dying. It is hard to see sunshine in a storm. You are going to face detours, roadblocks, wrecks, and unexpected things.

But just as I always say, never lose hope. Try to find light when you are lost. Look for the beauty in a storm because you are in control of how you see your life and how you determine it. Never let your circumstances influence your attitude because only you should decide what choices you want to make. I encourage you to take control of your life and define it according to your own rules.

Whenever you feel lost, confused, or in a storm, I want you to think about the consequences of those setbacks or losses in your life. Stand up and face the rejection. Don't let yourself be intimidated by anything. Believe that you can do it, raise the bar on yourself, and say that you have that courage in you.

When your life is running smoothly, and suddenly things turn upside down and everything turns into a mess, what is it that will let you get back on your feet again? It's your faith in yourself and your belief in positive things. Do you want to be that person who would show up and still stand strong no matter what and how the circumstances would be? Commit to yourself that you will stay concrete in your decisions.

Your character is not something you inherit. It is something that you build every day. Learn to build a strong character so that when failures fall on you, and you find yourself amid crises, you are ready to fight them. Face your fears and fight them off for your happiness, rather than quitting and being a victim. Don't take the easy path and squander this life; instead, live it with fortitude.

You might have been wondering if there is any explanation for why you're always going through hardships in your life. It seems to you that whatever pain and hurt you are going through don't make any sense. But let me tell you that just when you think that nothing makes sense, it all means that it's time for you to fight harder. It is time for you to stand tall, lift your head to the sky, and believe that you will overcome it.

There is always something good hiding beneath the bad circumstances. You just need to find it yourself. Don't lose hope because good things take time to happen. Never let your disabilities or shortcomings get in your way. Instead, turn them around into the greatness of success. Never let your weaknesses overcome you; in fact, make good use of them and stay strong.

What if you can't see, but you are trying to ride an avalanche of water? Imagine that you are trying to tear down the assaulting waves to keep your boat above the surface just by the sound of your guide, the waves, and your boat. What is it that still keeps you floating? It is your belief in yourself.

Have faith in what you can do and even in what you cannot do. Find the good in the bad, find light in the darkness, and even find happiness in your sorrows. This is the biggest secret to a successful life.

Erik Weihenmeyer, an American athlete and motivational speaker, said that the most torturous aspect of life is when we become pioneers, and we reach out beyond convention and discover the unexpected ways between what others may see as impossible and what we believe in our hearts to be fully possible.

Whenever you hit a barrier, it is time for you to break yourself free of that confinement and move out. Because if you attempt to give in and accept all the oppositions, then they would take over you, and you would never be able to stand up again. Open up your mind and try out new things because this is your time to set an example, despite your flaws.

I was once sitting in my armchair thinking about what life had thrown at me and how I had been able to come out clean. I realized that if I had given in to that state of despair and anxiety where I almost killed myself, there would have been no Gary Erneus, a visually impaired entrepreneur and lawyer now. I realized that this was only possible through courage and my faith in myself because I never gave up and stood my ground.

While I was thinking about all of this, I imagined in my mind how an ant tries to climb up a wall but falls on the first attempt. But she is more courageous than humans because she never stops there and backs out. Instead, with that faith in herself, she tries over and over again to climb that wall, and at last, she turns out to be successful. The same ant that was crawling on the floor is now climbing up the wall. Just because she never cared about the obstacles, she made several attempts to reach the wall. And at last, she was successful.

As humans, we feel pain and get hurt, but what we crave are victory and triumph. If only we didn't fear anyone and created our own destinies, we would be able to conquer the world. And, then, you will see that your hands are full of the rarest pearls.

Chapter 10
Wear the Cape and Fly!

"However difficult life may seem; there is always something
you can do and succeed at."
-Stephen Hawking

During my adolescence, I realized and learned that difficulties in life are inevitable. This idea has since been a constant in my world. I've always tried to overcome the challenges in my life, despite my disability. No matter what came my way or whatever life threw at me, I decided to fight those circumstances off just with my willpower. All of this was only possible because I believed in myself. I knew I could possibly do everything for myself without depending on anyone else, and it was a wonderful feeling. I had entirely been successful in claiming in front of ordinary people that I was not dependent on anyone as I attempted to manage things myself, which is one of the reasons I believe I turned out to be so efficient. I created ways to follow the standard method of life so that people don't look down on me or consider me an outcast. Even when my grades were below average, I aimed to fashion innovative strategies to help myself out.

I had been forced to live life as a blind person and be dependent on other people for help. But luckily, I refused to do so because I never accepted that I was any less than the normal ones. This courage, however, turned me into the person that I am today—the resilient one. My faith in my capabilities had given me the courage, motivation, drive, and intention to achieve anything and everything in life.

After getting into the vending machine business, I started volunteering at the shelter for needy people who needed my help. The main purpose of my independent services was to motivate others to never give up.

I volunteered to speak to graduating students at the Lighthouse in Sarasota. I spoke to a group of visually impaired students to show them they can succeed in life despite their disability. During my voluntary services, I also had the privilege to change someone's life by encouraging and motivating them.

I also volunteered to talk to people who were struggling with suicidal thoughts due to injuries or certain events in their lives that left them deprived of living a normal life. I loved getting to know people who were going through the worst times of their lives due to injuries and circumstances, just like I did. I wanted to console them and tried to enter their lives as a ray of hope, telling them that their good days were right around the corner.

One day, at the end of my lecture at a motivational session for disabled people, a blind man came up to me. We sat down in the corner of the hotel lobby to talk. He told me that he was going through a tough time. I was successful in gaining his confidence, which made him talk more comfortably to me during the next few minutes. I told him that he could be at ease while talking to me. He could open up and share his thoughts with me, whatever he was going through.

At first, he hesitated. He had come up to me because he felt inspired. As soon as the moment came when we both sat down on purpose to talk everything out, he started feeling shy. I then made him feel relaxed at first and then acquired his complete attention through my encouraging words.

His name was Adrian Jones, and he was disappointed by his failures and was on the verge of taking his own life.

He was thinking about committing suicide because he was gradually losing his sight for some medical reasons. He told me that he owned a jewelry business in Ottawa, Canada. He was quite a rich businessman and was floating in treasures.

But then, some of his acquaintances started becoming envious of his growing success and began plotting against him. He was a multimillionaire with ample and substantial resources. He was surrounded by men who were always there for his protection.

One day, while he was coming out of his office, a few people tried to take him down with a gunshot. Luckily, he was saved, but the bullet went closely past his left eye, giving him a deep wound. The person then went into a coma for almost a month as his condition was severe.

Adrian lived alone and wasn't married, so there was no one behind him from his family. When he came out of the coma, the doctors examined him and found out that he was soon going to lose his sight, first from his left eye and then gradually from the other. Adrian was devastated to know that he was going to be blind in the near future.

Although his business kept running in his absence, some of his subordinates tried to snag him with certain fraudulent activities. For the days that he was out of the office, his employees kept mishandling his business. By the time he resumed work after getting discharged from the hospital, things had turned upside down. He was robbed by his own employees, who deceived him.

Adrian was devastated once again, as life had been harsh on him one more time as if the injury wasn't bad enough. He hadn't recovered from his last, and the next one hit him like a giant rock. This major financial loss tore him to shreds.

I heard his story very calmly and was moved by his harsh experiences. I then narrated to him my success story and told him how I coped with hurdles on my way to success. I told him that these rough patches in life are inevitable.

I told him that we could not escape the hard times that were already written for us. It is just that we need to cope with them tactfully and try to get out of those problems. I motivated him that it doesn't matter even if he goes blind. All he would have to do is declare his strength and faith in himself.

That man was impressed by my encouraging words, which helped him turn his negative and suicidal thoughts into positive endeavors. Soon, he registered at a school for the disabled and changed the direction of his life.

I also volunteered to speak to children in different high schools across the country regarding the abuse of drugs.

I wanted to enlighten them so that they would know how severely drugs can affect their lives. I wanted to let those children, who had recently stepped into their teenage years, know the fallout that drugs could cause them. In my speeches to the students of high schools, I tried to teach them how substance abuse and addiction can make their lives miserable in the long run.

I mostly catered to teenage children who were capable of easily falling prey to the use of drugs while catching the habits from their surroundings. I tried to tell them that addiction and drug use could ruin their future and put obstacles in the way of their success. This was my volunteer work for the FDN Foundation, which worked with the motto of having a drug-free world. This foundation is also used to help politicians raise funds and go on the radio to discuss embarking on voluntary services. Working with the FDN Foundation in their voluntary work project, I always tried to motivate people to vote and make their voice count.

In the future, I want to use this book to inspire, motivate, empower, and coach people on how to use their inner will and their mind to succeed in life, regardless of the disabilities and obstacles they might face. I will also speak through my other books and attempt to coach people on how to succeed without getting affected by the problems in their lives.

I aim to use this book to speak to kids and teenagers about ways to overcome their disabilities and to use them as a platform to move forward in life by excelling at what they can do best. I would also love to teach them how to learn from their disabilities instead of cursing their lives.

My foremost intention in my writings is to teach the needy people out there that their disabilities or shortcomings are not a problem. Rather, they can still go to school and obtain any degree that they put their mind into.

I would also address, through my writings, the depressed souls who are facing anxiety and hopelessness. I want to tell them not to give up because depression is only a sickness and not the end of the world.

Through my experiences in life, I have learned that sometimes you have to fail before you fly, just like I did. I was once a failure and was about to end my life. But then I saw a ray of light, giving me hope for a new start. I never let my disability come in my way of success as I fought it.

Similarly, I would advise you to awaken the greatness within you and never let it go away or let someone else take it away from you. In fact, make use of your best skills to live a contented life.

Imagine if you die today, what stories, what dreams, what talents or gifts would die with you? Most people don't use their imaginations or dreams anymore. It is because they have been through rejections in life several times. Most people allow life to control them and their circumstances. But I would never advise you to let that happen to you. Because if you let life control you, then nothing might change in your life, and you'll learn later in life that it was all for nothing.

Instead, just look into the future and emphasize the things that you want to create for yourself. If you want to make your dreams come true, then you need to stay focused on them. Choose your path and follow it. Never settle for this because you know that this is not it for your life. You know that you deserve more and better.

It is necessary for you to have your dream on which you will have to work. You will also need to develop yourself and go for what is yours in the universe. The major key to reaching your dream and living up to your greatness is YOU. Only *you* can make things happen in your life. All it takes is your courage and faith in yourself. But this would require your personal responsibility and your devoted attention toward your aims.

You need to remind yourself that you need powers and talents within you that you haven't even reached yet. Remember that whatever dream or idea you have, it has been transcended upon you; therefore, you need to fulfill it—it is your calling. There is no guarantee that those who are now down on their luck can never get back up again. In fact, no man in this world can assure that.

The famous poet William Ernest Henley once said, "I am the master of my soul; I am the captain of my faith." So, it is only you who can bring about change in your life. Find out what it is that you want, and then go after it, as your life depends on it. Never wait for tomorrow to come, because there is no guarantee that it will show up. So many people were here yesterday, but they are not here today.

Similarly, there were a lot of opportunities yesterday that are not here today. Life doesn't guarantee anything. But there is one guarantee: if you don't take action today, there will be no outcome tomorrow. The only outcome would be that you didn't achieve what you wanted.

Many people think that failure is a step backward. But that is not the case. Actually, failure is a step forward in the right direction. Every time you fail, you learn something. Failure means progress in every sense of the word. Your dreams come to you for a reason. It is up to you to either act on them or just abandon them.

Having experienced frequent changes in different surroundings, I can now adapt without compromising what is important to me while learning from each new turn of events.

Every situation life had thrown at me had its differences, but they all molded me to want to help other people not give up during their most challenging circumstances. I had the motivation and a definite aim to succeed. Underneath all the hardships, there still lies something more critical. I believe who I am today is immeasurably more important than what I have endured in life.

www.ingramcontent.com/pod-product-compliance
Lightning Source LLC
Chambersburg PA
CBHW061524050726
47503CB00016B/2723